MISS BUNSEN'S SCHOOL FOR BRILLIANT GIRLS

Penny for Your Thoughts

MISS BUNSEN'S SCHOOL FOR BRILLIANT GIRLS

Penny for Your Thoughts

Erica-Jane Waters

Albert Whitman & Company
Chicago, Illinois

Library of Congress Cataloging-in-Publication data
is on file with the publisher.

Printed in the United States of America
10 9 8 7 6 5 4 3 2 1 LB 24 23 22 21 20 19

Design by Aphelandra Messer

For more information about Albert Whitman & Company,
visit our website at www.albertwhitman.com.

For Daddy,
engineer extraordinaire

Chapter 1

"Ouch!" Halinka shrieked as the double-decker school bus bumped over a pothole, causing Millie's enormous tool kit to fall from the luggage compartment above and land directly on her head.

"Good thing you've got a thick head of hair to protect you," said Pearl, smiling as she and Millie helped Halinka pull a wrench out of her curls.

"Can you put this monstrosity somewhere more secure?" Halinka grumbled, passing

Millie her heavy bag.

"I know I'm overprepared," Millie said, "but you never know what you're going to need, or when you're going to need it."

"Overprepared!" Halinka guffawed. "You've got enough stuff in that rucksack to prepare the whole school to traverse the Himalayas!"

"Okay, maybe the skis are a little unnecessary, but it's better to be sure." Millie tightened the rope that fastened her old-fashioned wooden skis to her bag and shoved it back up into the overhead compartment, clonking Halinka on the head for the second time.

"Well, I prefer to just wing it. Travel light. There's always something lying around that I can improvise with," Halinka said as she pulled a piece of gum from the back of the seat in front of them and popped it into her mouth.

Pearl and Millie were having trouble controlling their expressions of disgust when they all heard a crackle and a loud whistling sound.

"Whoops! Sorry, girls," said Miss Bunsen as she tapped the microphone strapped to her head with one hand while trying to steer the bus with the other.

"I do apologize for the

last-minute school trip! There was no time to call an assembly, you see, as I only just found the letter. It was the squirrels, you see. They had hidden it in one of their nests and…"

One of the girls in the front seat cleared her throat in an exaggerated fashion.

"Oh, I'm going off track," Miss Bunsen muttered, causing a brief panic before everyone realized she was not talking about the country road they were traveling along.

"So, the letter," Miss Bunsen continued. "There was a letter that was only sent out to the most prestigious of schools—our glorious school included, of course—inviting us to take part in a mystery maze adventure."

The Bunseners aboard the bus looked at one another dubiously.

"Who was the letter from, Miss Bunsen?" Penelope, the head girl, asked.

"Well, it didn't really say. All part of the mystery!" Miss Bunsen replied, sounding a little nervous now herself.

"What's the prize?" Halinka called down the bus from her seat in the back.

"Well, erm, oh dear. I never did ask, but I do know it's a large and undisclosed sum of money. Money that we desperately need to fix our crumbling school."

"I don't think any amount of money will ever possibly be enough to fix our school," a quiet little voice said.

"Sophie Syntax!" Miss Bunsen chided. "That is *not* the attitude of a Bunsener! Let's all just do our best as we always do and charge on ahead!"

The bus began to hum with whispers as the Bunseners questioned where they were going and why Miss Bunsen didn't have any information.

The sky darkened, and spots of rain began to dot the front windshield of the bus. Miss Bunsen fumbled for the wipers, only to turn on the hazard lights and sound the horn instead.

"This is ridiculous," Millie scoffed, folding her arms and staring out the window at the fields passing by.

"What's the matter, Millie?" Pearl asked in a concerned tone.

"Millie doesn't like surprises," Halinka said

as she stood up to get a look at the route ahead.

"Halinka, sit down! You know we're not allowed to stand up when the bus is moving," Millie scolded.

"All right, all right," Halinka said, thumping down into her seat again, a little taken aback by her usually timid friend's sudden outburst.

Pearl looked at Millie through narrowed eyes and gave her a gentle nudge.

"Hey, what's up? It's not like you to be grumpy."

Millie turned to her friends with a look on her face that neither of them had seen before. She was very serious.

"I just don't understand Miss Bunsen some-times," she began. "I mean, I love her, but she frustrates me. If our school is teeming with young scientists, engineers, designers, and inventors, why is it falling down? Would Miss Bunsen not be better off setting us the task of renovating the school? Then we wouldn't be off on a wild-goose chase to

goodness knows where. We could be heading for real danger, and all because Miss Bunsen hasn't looked into this properly."

Pearl put an arm around Millie.

"Millie, Miss Bunsen sees us as her own children! She loves us and would never want to burden us with building work. She believes that her school is a place of learning and creativity, where we should be free to explore our imaginations—not spend our days mending roofs. And Miss Bunsen would never put us in danger."

"Maybe not intentionally," Millie said darkly.

"Just thank your lucky nuts and bolts that 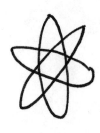 you don't have Miss Acid as your headmistress. Imagine how you'd feel if you went to Atom Academy!" Halinka removed her gum and placed it under the seat for later.

"And I'm sure they'll be there at this competition," said Pearl, rolling her eyes. "Not that they even need the prize money! They'll just turn up to show off their new state-of-the-art school bus with its tinted windows and heated leather seats."

Millie wriggled about uncomfortably on one of the bus's slatted wooden seats before turning to her friends once again.

"I just don't understand how she lets herself be guided by her feelings about things, when the practical solution is right in front of her. It's not scientific!"

"What's wrong with feelings?" Halinka asked sharply.

There was a long pause as Halinka and Pearl watched their friend turn back to look out the window, her breath misting it up and her finger doodling various trigonometric symbols.

They waited for Millie to answer, but she never did, too lost in her thoughts.

The rickety old bus carried on its bumpy journey with its occupants all excitedly discussing their upcoming adventure—all

but three. The silence that had fallen over the back seat of the bus was only broken by a loud clap of thunder and the screeching of brakes.

"Girls! We're here!"

Chapter 2

The bus came to an abrupt halt, causing hats, hockey sticks, and cheese and pickle sandwiches to shower down from the luggage racks.

A torrent of black boots clattered down the bus's spiral staircase as the top-floor Bunseners disembarked.

"Careful you don't slip!" Miss Bunsen shouted over the excited screams and laughter. "Brains has done a piddle!" Brains was Miss Bunsen's cat of uncertain age, whose body had been mostly replaced with metal plates, nuts, and bolts.

Pearl looked out the window at the crowd of girls gathered next to the bus, umbrellas jostling for space.

"Where are all the other schools?" she asked, breaking the silence among her friends.

"Maybe it's all part of the game?" Halinka mused as she shuffled her way down to the front of the bus.

"It would help if we had any information," Millie whispered.

"Come on, Millie, let's just go with it for now. It'll be fun," said Pearl, not entirely believing herself.

"Over here, ladies!"

Miss Bunsen was busy making her way toward a pair of large steel doors that fronted a deserted-looking warehouse.

"This place is weird. Something doesn't feel right," Millie said. Her raincoat and hood were secured tightly around her face, and her round glasses steamed up.

Pearl looked around. There was nothing to see for miles except power lines, scrubland, and thunderclouds. The warehouse was huge, made from concrete, and had no windows. Not for the first time, Pearl began to wonder if Millie was right.

"I guess all the other schools parked around the back?" she asked Halinka, hoping to get a little reassurance from her confident friend.

Halinka pulled a pencil from behind her ear and began chewing the end. "Something's off," she said finally. "I smell a squirrel."

"Don't you mean a rat?" Millie said. She raised her eyebrows at Halinka.

"No," Halinka said, raising her eyebrows right back at Millie. "I mean a squirrel. Lots of them, actually."

Sure enough, there was a small gathering of squirrels scampering about by the doors of the ominous warehouse.

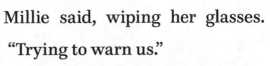

"I think they're trying to tell us something," Millie said, wiping her glasses. "Trying to warn us."

"Now who's being ridiculous?" Halinka retorted, but before the conversation could go any further, the warehouse doors slowly opened, revealing a huge sign. It read WELCOME TO THE IMPOSSIBLE MAZE in big, bold letters.

"Oh, thank goodness for that!" Pearl let out a sigh of relief. The three friends looked at each other and laughed.

"We were worrying about nothing," Halinka said as she slipped her arms around her friends' shoulders. "Let's do this!"

Miss Bunsen led her students inside the warehouse and into a large room with a blue velvet curtain at one end.

"Girls! Let's please be quiet, as I'm quite sure someone will be here to greet us any minute."

The room was silent, apart from the dripping of wet umbrellas.

"Any minute now."

The light in the room began to slowly dim.

"Is this a maze or the movies?" asked Halinka as her friends' faces disappeared in the darkness.

"I'm a bit scared," Millie whimpered.

1 **H** Hydrogen								
3 **Li** Lithium	4 **Be** Beryllium							
11 **Na** Sodium	12 **Mg** Magnesium							

19 **K** Potassium	20 **Ca** Calcium	21 **Sc** Scandium	22 **Ti** Titanium	23 **V** Vanadium	24 **Cr** Chromium	25 **Mn** Manganese	26 **Fe** Iron	27 **Co** Cobalt
37 **Rb** Rubidium	38 **Sr** Strontium	39 **Y** Yttrium	40 **Zr** Zirconium	41 **Nb** Niobium	42 **Mo** Molybdenum	43 **Tc** Technetium	44 **Ru** Ruthenium	45 **Rh** Rhodium
55 **Cs** Caesium	56 **Ba** Barium	57–71	72 **Hf** Hafnium	73 **Ta** Tantalum	74 **W** Tungsten	75 **Re** Rhenium	76 **Os** Osmium	77 **Ir** Iridium
87 **Fr** Francium	88 **Ra** Radium	89–103	104 **Rf** Rutherfordium	105 **Db** Dubnium	106 **Sg** Seaborgium	107 **Bh** Bohrium	108 **Hs** Hassium	109 **Mt** Meitnerium

57 **La** Lanthanum	58 **Ce** Cerium	59 **Pr** Praseodymium	60 **Nd** Neodymium	61 **Pm** Promethium	62 **Sm** Samarium	63 **Eu** Europium
89 **Ac** Actinium	90 **Th** Thorium	91 **Pa** Protactinium	92 **U** Uranium	93 **Np** Neptunium	94 **Pu** Plutonium	95 **Am** Americium

Pearl fumbled around and found Millie and Halinka's hands. "Don't worry, it's all part of the maze."

Soon the room was in almost complete darkness, with only the blue velvet curtain still visible in the dim light. The girls watched as it slowly drew up toward the ceiling, revealing a glass touch screen with a large table lit up upon it.

"The periodic table," Millie whispered. "A

								² He Helium
			⁵ B Boron	⁶ C Carbon	⁷ N Nitrogen	⁸ O Oxygen	⁹ F Flourine	¹⁰ Ne Neon
			¹³ Al Aluminum	¹⁴ Si Silicon	¹⁵ P Phosphorus	¹⁶ S Sulfur	¹⁷ Cl Chlorine	¹⁸ Ar Argon
²⁸ Ni Nickel	²⁹ Cu Copper	³⁰ Zn Zinc	³¹ Ga Gallium	³² Ge Germanium	³³ As Arsenic	³⁴ Se Selenium	³⁵ Br Bromine	³⁶ Kr Krypton
⁴⁶ Pd Palladium	⁴⁷ Ag Silver	⁴⁸ Cd Cadmium	⁴⁹ In Indium	⁵⁰ Sn Tin	⁵¹ Sb Antimony	⁵² Te Tellurium	⁵³ I Iodine	⁵⁴ Xe Xenon
⁷⁸ Pt Platinum	⁷⁹ Au Gold	⁸⁰ Hg Mercury	⁸¹ Tl Thallium	⁸² Pb Lead	⁸³ Bi Bismuth	⁸⁴ Po Polonium	⁸⁵ At Astatine	⁸⁶ Rn Radon
¹¹⁰ Ds Darmstadtium	¹¹¹ Rg Roentgenium	¹¹² Cn Copernicium	¹¹³ Nh Nihonium	¹¹⁴ Fl Flerovium	¹¹⁵ Mc Moscovium	¹¹⁶ Lv Livermorium	¹¹⁷ Ts Tennessine	¹¹⁸ Og Oganesson

⁶⁴ Gd Gadolinium	⁶⁵ Tb Terbium	⁶⁶ Dy Dysprosium	⁶⁷ Ho Holmium	⁶⁸ Er Erbium	⁶⁹ Tm Thulium	⁷⁰ Yb Ytterbium	⁷¹ Lu Lutetium
⁹⁶ Cm Curium	⁹⁷ Bk Berkelium	⁹⁸ Cf Californium	⁹⁹ Es Einsteinium	¹⁰⁰ Fm Fermium	¹⁰¹ Md Mendelevium	¹⁰² No Nobelium	¹⁰³ Lr Lawrencium

perfect table of chemical elements, along with their atomic numbers and electronic configurations, all in one place. Don't you just love looking at it?"

"We do, but probably not as much as you do," said Pearl with a friendly laugh.

"Look at that," said Halinka, pointing to a neon sign flickering to life above the touch screen.

"Ah, at last." Miss Bunsen cheered, ruining the hushed, magical atmosphere somewhat. "Now, who wants to guess what our next step should be?"

The room was quiet. Then a little voice piped up.

"We can't read the sign, Miss Bunsen," said a first-year girl.

"This doesn't make any sense!" cried another.

"Well, we need to get started somehow!" Miss Bunsen said, her voice sounding slightly panicked. "Can anyone read the sign?"

"I can."

Halinka stepped forward.

"Miss Bunsen, do you happen to have a compact in your handbag?"

Miss Bunsen rummaged around in her enormous handbag, pulling out a wrench, a pair of rubber gloves, a potted plant, and a fishing rod before handing Halinka the small mirror.

Halinka turned her back to the sign, flipped open the compact, and viewed the swirly neon writing from the reflection.

"It's back to front!" Pearl said, looking at Millie's neon-lit face for a sign that her friend was impressed by Halinka's smart thinking. Millie still looked worried.

Halinka read out the backwards sign's message:

"Where are you from?
No time to fidget,
To solve the wall,
You must find the correct digit."

Halinka stepped back to Millie and Pearl.
"Isn't Halinka a genius, Millie?" said Pearl.

But Millie just pulled her notebook out of her rucksack and began to make notes. "Shhh, we need to work this out," she said.

Halinka looked at her friend and frowned.

"Look! What's that?" squeaked a tiny Bunsener at the front of the crowd.

"It's a keypad!" Millie said excitedly.

"What does this mean?" Pearl asked, looking confused as she stared at the big, square buttons with the numbers zero to nine glowing in the dim light.

"I think we need to punch a number into the keypad," Halinka suggested. "'The correct digit,' like it says on the sign."

"But what digit?" Pearl asked as a wave of whispers floated around the room. The Bunseners were all trying to figure out the puzzle.

"I've got it! I've worked it out!" Millie cried, nearly knocking over several small Bunseners in her rush to get to the front of the room.

She swirled around and grabbed an umbrella from one of the girls to use as a pointing stick.

"So—where are we from?" she continued.

"Miss Bunsen's!" came an enthusiastic roar from the girls.

"Right. So maybe we need to spell out BUNSEN using the elements from the periodic table! Then we take the atomic numbers from those elements and add them up, giving us the correct digit!"

Millie began pointing at the screen with the umbrella.

"Boron is 5, uranium, 92, nitrogen, 7, selenium, 34, and then nitrogen again, so another 7...It adds up to 145! Let's punch it in, and then we can get to the next stage!"

Millie began to enter the digits into the keypad. She tried several times, but nothing happened.

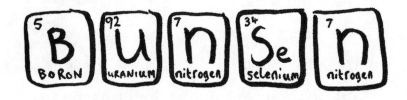

"It's not working!" She sighed, frustrated.

"Maybe that's the wrong sequence of elements!" Halinka called out. "We might just need to change something around."

Millie's shoulders dropped. "Halinka, you simply *cannot* change the periodic table. It's set in stone! Well, glass in this case."

"Nothing is ever set in stone, Millie. Look, the

neon sign is backwards, right?"

The girls and Miss Bunsen all nodded along in agreement.

"Then the sequence we need is boron, 5, uranium, 92, nitrogen, 7, sulfur, 16, and neon, 10."

"BUNSNE is not a word!" Millie said impatiently.

Halinka pointed to the neon sign above their heads.

"The neon sign is backwards. I think that means we need to use the symbol for neon backwards!"

"EN!" shouted the whole school in unison.

"And those elements' numbers add up to 130. Let's punch that in!"

Millie typed the new digits into the keypad and waited.

The room suddenly lit up with a golden light,

and a fanfare of trumpets played out around their ears.

All the students cheered, excited to move on to the next stage of the maze.

"It worked!" Millie said gleefully.

"Sometimes it's worth thinking outside the box, Millie," Halinka said.

"Your calculations made sense too," Pearl added, noticing the small frown on Millie's face. "It was tricky."

But no sooner had she spoken than the whole room was plunged once again into darkness.

Chapter 3

A crackling noise reverberated around the dark room, and then a voice reached them through the gloom.

"Welcome to the Impossible Maze," it said.

Millie felt Halinka sidle up closer to her; she could tell it was her from the smell of gum.

"Who is this?" Miss Bunsen called out. "Reveal yourself! My girls are becoming frightened."

Suddenly, a beam of light flooded the dark room as a pair of doors slid open to reveal a long corridor flanked by glass-walled rooms. Each room had various puzzles and conundrums to solve. There were cogs and wheels, pulleys and counterweights to understand. Some rooms had symbols and ancient hieroglyphs painted on the walls, and the floors were covered in sand.

"Whoa!" Pearl whooped as she caught up with Halinka and Millie. "This maze is awesome!"

The students entered the corridor, and the doors slid shut again behind them.

The crackly voice once again came over the speakers.

"Well, congratulations, Miss Bunsen's School for Brilliant Girls—you have officially made it past the first puzzle! Now let's see how brilliant you really are…"

A wave of excitement fluttered through the girls. They were ready for the fun part of the maze to begin.

"Kindly form a line, four deep. The line will begin with the first-year students and end with the final-year girls. The girls to the left and right of you will be your team."

The Bunseners shuffled themselves about until a tidy queue had formed. Pearl, Halinka, and Millie were side by side at the very back with Miss Bunsen.

The voice continued. "Look in front of you, and you will see a large hourglass. This is how long you have to solve each room. If you haven't solved the room before the timer runs out, you will be locked in...forever!"

The schoolgirls all giggled and clung to one another's arms.

"Ooh, drama," Halinka said sarcastically, trying to look unimpressed.

"Team one—GO!"

The door to the first room flew open, and the first four girls in the line dashed inside. The hourglass turned 180 degrees, and the sand inside began to fall.

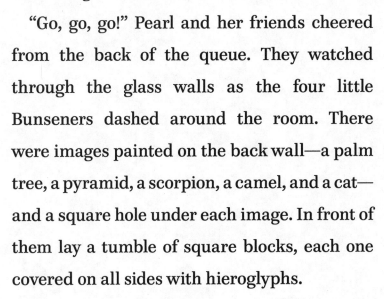

"Go, go, go!" Pearl and her friends cheered from the back of the queue. They watched through the glass walls as the four little Bunseners dashed around the room. There were images painted on the back wall—a palm tree, a pyramid, a scorpion, a camel, and a cat—and a square hole under each image. In front of them lay a tumble of square blocks, each one covered on all sides with hieroglyphs.

The girls soon figured out what they needed to do. They quickly began to search for the correct hieroglyph to match the picture, before sliding the block into place underneath. When the last block was pushed into place, the images lit up.

"We did it, we did it!" the girls cheered. Pearl, Millie, and Halinka cheered along with them.

"TOO BAD!" the voice boomed over the speaker. "You were just out of time. Next team!"

The next door in the corridor swung open, and in went a new group of Bunseners, the door locking shut behind them.

"Come on, you can do it!" cheered the rest of the girls outside.

This time, the team was faced with a room painted deep blue. The walls and ceiling were covered in twinkly lights.

"Oh wow," Pearl gasped. "It looks so pretty! I wish that was our challenge."

The floor was a mass of balls of all different sizes in every color imaginable. Hanging from the ceiling were lengths of golden string, each with a tiny hook on the end.

The team soon figured out that they were supposed to re-create the solar system. They began frantically searching for the planets among the heap of balls.

"I found Jupiter!"

"I found Mars!"

"And I found the Earth!"

The Bunseners placed the largest ball, which was golden yellow, on the first hook, followed by Mercury, Venus, and Earth.

The other students watched as the team hesitated, trying to remember what came after Earth. But soon enough Mars, Jupiter, Saturn, and Neptune were all hooked up in place.

They hurriedly began to hang the planets in order on the hooks above, and before long, the solar system was complete.

"There's something missing," a member of the team said, realizing the door hadn't unlocked.

There was still a little bit of sand left in the hourglass.

"Found it!" came a little voice as one of the team pulled out a ring from the balls and fastened it to Saturn.

But again, even though the puzzle was solved, the door remained locked as the hourglass emptied, leaving the team trapped inside.

"This doesn't seem fair," Halinka said, turning to her friends and Miss Bunsen. "I'm sure that they completed that task in time."

"Yes, I'm quite sure they solved that puzzle before the time ran out too," Miss Bunsen said. She looked a little more befuddled than usual.

Team after team entered the long row of rooms—and team after team remained locked inside their puzzle chamber.

"Excuse me!" Miss Bunsen called out into the air, sounding unsure of how one was supposed to address a voice that was seemingly coming from nowhere. "This doesn't seem terribly fair—all but three of my girls are locked in."

Miss Bunsen looked in despair at Pearl, Halinka, and Millie. "How can we possibly win with no rooms left anyway?"

The voice came once again.

"MWAH-HA-HA-HA! It's not called the Impossible Maze for no reason, Miss Bunsen. Never fear, I have one more puzzle for you to solve. I have left the best for the best.

"ENTER the final phase!"

Chapter 4

Pearl, Halinka, and Millie clung to one another as Miss Bunsen nervously fiddled with her earrings.

The lights in the glass corridor dimmed to nearly total darkness, and the entire end wall of the corridor opened to reveal yet another room.

"Look up, up to the sky," the voice whispered in a menacing tone.

Miss Bunsen and the students slowly looked up, scared of what they might see.

"What is it?" Millie whimpered. "I can't see.

My glasses don't see that far!"

"It looks like some kind of golden lift," Pearl said, straining to see herself.

"It's awfully high up!" Miss Bunsen said.

"I think that's the problem we need to solve," Halinka said determinedly.

"CORRECT!" came the voice. "This is the golden elevator of glory. Find a way to bring it down to this level, step inside, and you will be elevated to riches beyond your wildest dreams!"

"Sounds easy enough," Halinka said, shrugging her shoulders. "All we need to do is fling this up to hit the button." She pulled a billiard ball out of her bag and began marching toward the opening to the room.

"Halinka, stop!" Millie called after her friend.

"Come on," Halinka said as she turned back for a moment. "What are you waiting for?"

Millie pulled out her flashlight from her tool bag and switched it to infrared before shining it into the room.

"Look," she said gravely.

Miss Bunsen, Brains, and the three girls walked slowly toward the room.

"Well, this changes things a bit," Halinka

said, looking at the web of infrared beams that had been revealed by Millie's torch.

"Yes, yes it does." The voice laughed menacingly. "Just one of those beams gets touched, even by a feather, and the whole maze is over and you lose. Now enter the room."

After they were inside it, a door slid slowly shut behind them, leaving just a tiny space for the team to stand without touching any of the beams.

"Look at how tightly packed these beams are," Millie said, feeling defeated. "There's not even enough space for Brains to squeeze through."

"There must be a way we can get that elevator down!" Pearl looked at Miss Bunsen, who was standing in front of Brains to stop him from running off and making them lose the challenge.

"It's impossible," Millie said, pulling a protractor and various other measuring devices out of her tool bag. "There is no direct tunnel through the beams for us to throw the ball through to hit that button on the elevator. There are no holes or gaps large enough for us to climb through without touching a beam and losing the game. We've lost. It's impossible to get from here to there. We cannot get from A to B."

"Nothing is impossible!" Halinka said, grabbing her logical friend by the shoulders. "Logic will get you from one A to B, but there's a whole other world between A and B. What you need is ingenuity."

Pearl listened with interest to her friends' argument.

"Halinka," Millie said with a sigh, "there is nothing between A and B. You can't change the alphabet."

"Just watch me," Halinka said, pulling a pencil from behind her ear. "Empty your bags."

Halinka began to draw on the back of the door.

"We are here—A. And we need to get the button pressed on the elevator—B.

"There are plenty of gaps and spaces in

between those infrared beams. We just need to do it in stages."

"Like a Rube Goldberg machine!" Pearl clapped excitedly.

"Exactly!" Halinka said.

"Oh, you are clever girls!" cheered Miss Bunsen. "How shall we start?"

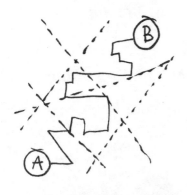

"Millie," Halinka said, pointing to the diagram beginning to form on the back of the door. "You are the logical one. You are a whiz at trigonometry, angles, and all that stuff. I need you to measure a path through the beams."

Millie nodded thoughtfully and began to map out a scaled-down version of the beams on the door.

"Pearl, you are our top designer. We need to

get this billiard ball to hit that button on that elevator."

"No can do," Millie interrupted. "According to my calculations, the spaces in between the beams at the top are so small you could barely fit a penny though them."

"Hmm," said Pearl. "I could design something like a catapult to get a penny through those initial beams, or maybe a blast of air pressure would get it going fast enough to move the billiard ball." She began rummaging about in the pile of stuff on the floor that had been emptied out of the bags. "Some serious velocity is what we need."

Halinka tied several lengths of shoelaces together. She chewed her way through six packs of gum astonishingly quickly, then smooshed the pink goo onto the ends of the laces before shooting them straight up above their heads by blowing each one through a straw.

"There!" she said, grinning. "Our first point of construction is in place."

The three girls looked up at the laces dangling from the ceiling and got to work tying books, playing cards, and Millie's old skis to them, raising them up carefully to avoid the beams. Then they slid them along toward the elevator, using shoes as weights.

"I knew my skis were an essential thing to pack!" Millie said. She gently pulled on a long length of yarn, heaving up a row of dominoes that had been lying flat until that point.

The girls had carefully rigged a network of playing cards, cans of soda ready to pop, and batteries with their polar ends wired together to create a boost of energy, all meticulously slid, pushed, and wiggled into place so as not to touch the infrared beams.

"Do you think this will work?" Pearl asked nervously as she put the final touches on the machine.

"I've worked everything out to a millionth of a millimeter," Millie replied. "As long as the ball keeps gathering momentum, there will be enough power behind it for it to weave its way through the beams and hit that button."

"I hope your calculations are right, Millie. If anything even so much as brushes against one of those beams, that's it. Game over." Pearl kissed the penny for luck and held it in its starting place.

"Ready?" she asked, looking up at the others one more time.

Everyone nodded, Brains's neck squeaking as he did so. "He needs oiling," Miss Bunsen explained.

Pearl took a deep breath and let the penny roll down the first cardboard tube.

Chapter 5

The penny rolled perfectly out of the tube, knocking down a row of dominoes, the last of which set the billiard ball off on its journey. It slowly made its way along one of Millie's skis before dropping off the end onto a spring-set spoon, which launched the ball into a handkerchief sling. The billiard ball's weight in the sling triggered a hockey stick to swing and hit the ball straight up into a mill wheel made of cards, which spun the ball onto Millie's other ski. Another set of dominoes slowed the ball's

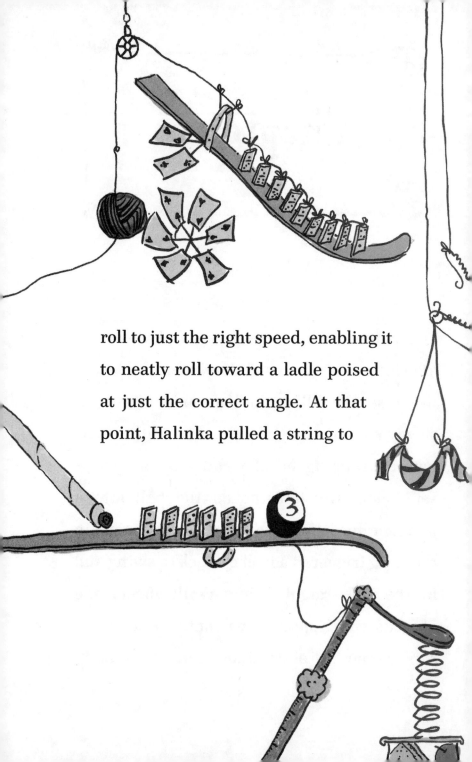

roll to just the right speed, enabling it
to neatly roll toward a ladle poised
at just the correct angle. At that
point, Halinka pulled a string to

drop a pineapple onto the ladle's handle, shooting the ball off on its final route to hit the elevator button.

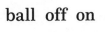

"Please work, please work, please work," Millie chanted, one eye shut tight. Her flashlight pointed toward the action so the beams were visible.

The girls and Miss Bunsen watched as the ball shot through the gaps in the infrared beams and hit the button square on.

"Yes!" Halinka and Pearl and Millie cried in unison as the beams all disappeared.

"The elevator is coming down!" Miss Bunsen

said excitedly, squeezing Brains a little too tightly.

"What's that smell?" Millie asked.

"Excitement." Halinka snorted, looking at Brains in disgust.

Slowly the elevator reached the floor, and the doors pinged open.

"Oh, girls, I'm so very proud of you. You solved the maze! We've won!" Miss Bunsen shrilled with delight.

"Come on, then, what are we waiting for?" Halinka said as she pulled everyone into the lift. "Let's go get our prize and get back to school!"

The doors slid shut, and they were greeted by quiet, tinkling music.

"Loving the tunes," Pearl said with a giggle.

"Wait," said Millie, suddenly

looking concerned. "I thought we were supposed to be going up."

"Millie's right," Pearl replied. "It feels like
we're going down."

The music abruptly ended. As the elevator
screeched to a stop, Miss Bunsen and the girls
could hear the voice laughing over the speaker
system.

"I don't know what's going on
here, but I don't like it!" Halinka
said as she furiously pressed the
door-open button.

Finally, the doors of
the elevator slid apart,
and Miss Bunsen, Pearl,
Millie, and Halinka stepped out.

"Hooray!" "Bravo!" "Well done!"

A wave of cheers and clapping
sounded around them, and

as their eyes grew used to the dim, candlelit room, they could see the entire school waiting for them.

"What on earth is going on?" Pearl said to Miss Bunsen. "Have we won or not?"

"I'm not sure, Pearl, my dear. We were ushered down into this delightful room by our mystery-voice host." Miss Bunsen sounded as though she was a little fed up with the mystery voice.

"So where's the prize?" Halinka said, crossing her arms and chewing on her gum.

"AND I THOUGHT BUNSENERS WERE SUPPOSED TO BE SMART!" boomed the voice.

The entire school huddled together.

"Maybe you should watch this," the voice continued. "You see, the only prize is your school... and it's going to be all mine!"

Chapter 6

An image of Miss Bunsen's School for Brilliant Girls flickered up onto the wall of the room in which they were now standing.

"*No!*" Miss Bunsen gasped, dropping Brains to the floor with a clank. "What have you done to my beautiful school?"

All the students in the room began to gasp as they watched their beloved school being surrounded by bulldozers and excavators. A sign reading "Demolition Site" was propped up against the old, rusty railings.

"Who are you?" Miss Bunsen demanded. "Why are you doing this?"

"HA-HA-HA-HA HAAA!" cackled the mystery voice. "Don't you think it's a little late in the day to be asking who I am now? Would it not have been more sensible to check who I was before you brought all your students to this lonely, remote warehouse in the middle of nowhere?"

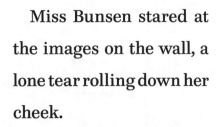

Miss Bunsen stared at the images on the wall, a lone tear rolling down her cheek.

"Listen to me," she replied sternly, wiping away the tear and straightening herself up to face the voice. "We are Bunseners, and we do things our way. I demand you let us out of here immediately."

"OR WHAT?" the voice bellowed.

Miss Bunsen fell silent, realizing she was helpless.

"I'll tell you what," the voice said. "I'll make you a deal."

Millie pulled on Miss Bunsen's arm. "Miss Bunsen, don't listen to the voice! This could all be a trick!"

Miss Bunsen gently removed Millie's hand from her arm.

"Go ahead, I'm listening."

The voice laughed softly.

"Legend has it, Miss Bunsen, that you have the ancient Tome of Thought hidden at your school. Give me the Tome, and the demolition stops. The bulldozers and excavators will be gone, and you will be free to go."

Pearl, Halinka, and Millie were now all pulling on Miss Bunsen's arm.

"Miss Bunsen," Pearl whispered frantically, "what is the Tome of Thought?"

Miss Bunsen leaned in a little closer to the three friends.

"The Tome of Thought is an ancient book from thousands of years ago. It has hand-written chapters from every great scientist, philosopher, inventor, and engineer in history.

They've all added to it over the years. It has been at our school ever since it was built. Some say that the authors of the Tome even sat in our medieval library, their bottoms resting on the wooden benches to write their pieces by candlelight."

Pearl, Halinka, and Millie listened in awe, their jaws dropped.

"You see," Miss Bunsen continued, "our school has been standing in the very same spot for many hundreds of years—maybe even thousands in one form or another. In its heyday, when money didn't matter in science, it was one of the grandest institutions in the world."

"But what about the book? The Tome? Why have you never mentioned it before?" Millie asked.

"Because, my dear Millie, to know about the

Tome is dangerous. I had to keep it a deep secret, as it is very special. It contains a vast range of information from the greatest thinkers and minds of our history. In the wrong hands, the

book is dangerous. That's why it's locked in the safe."

"Ah, thank you, Miss Bunsen!" the voice interrupted. "So not only are you aware of the book, but you have now given me its exact location."

The image on the wall flickered again and switched to a shot of a safe in Miss Bunsen's attic office.

"Oh, no—look!" Halinka pointed to the corner of the basement, where the hourglass had appeared again and was slowly losing sand from its top half.

"The code, please, Miss Bunsen. I haven't got

all day," said the voice. Miss Bunsen looked at her girls, their expressions frightened in the candlelight.

"The code you need is…"

"No, Miss Bunsen!" Halinka jumped up in front of her teacher. "Don't give in! We can get out of here ourselves."

"Yes," Pearl added. "We're Bunseners, remember?"

"Wait a minute," said Millie. "Are we going to be stuck in this horrible basement forever? At least if they get the book, we can all just go back to school."

"Millie!" Halinka shrieked. "Don't you care that the Tome could be dangerous in the wrong hands? And that it's been in our school for centuries?"

"I'm just being practical. Even if the book is important, is it more important than all of us and our well-being?" Her voice got quieter. "I want to get out of here."

"Time's nearly up!" the voice sneered.

Miss Bunsen looked once again at her girls, then up at the image as it switched back to the bulldozers moving closer and closer to her school.

"The code is 887190," Miss Bunsen said quickly. "Now, let us out."

"M WAH-HA-HA-HA-HAAAAAAA!" shrieked the voice, "Your naivety is so funny, it hurts. Goodbye, Miss Bunsen. Goodbye, Bunseners. Over and out."

Chapter 7

Miss Bunsen picked up Brains and walked over to a quiet corner of the room, her beloved Bunsen girls parting the way for her as she walked.

"What's Miss Bunsen doing?" Pearl whispered.

"I should think she is coming up with a most excellent plan to get us out of here," Halinka replied.

"I've never seen her like this," Pearl said, watching their teacher from across the room. "So quiet and thoughtful. Do you think she's okay?"

"You're very quiet too, Millie," Halinka said. "Are you okay?"

"I'm fine." Millie said, not looking up at either of her friends.

"Are you sure?" said Pearl, reaching over to move Millie's hair out of her face.

"Millie, you're crying!" said Halinka.

"Don't you see?" Millie said.

"See what?" Halinka replied, not sure if her friend was sad or cross.

"Miss Bunsen rushed into this without checking it out. She was so set on winning the money that she didn't wait a second to make sure it was safe. She was rash. She let her emotions override her logic, and now here we all are, locked in a warehouse. And the worst thing—the worst thing—is that not only has she let us down, but she has let all future Bunseners down because the Tome of Thought is no longer at our school. It is lost forever because Miss Bunsen didn't think before she jumped."

There was a long silence as Pearl and Halinka took in what their friend had just said.

Halinka let out a big puff of breath before replying. "And you would have done things better, would you, Miss Logical?"

Millie took off her glasses and wiped her eyes. "I was just saying that letting your emotions take over your senses is not a good idea, ever."

"Well, maybe you should be in charge of an entire school then, Millie. Maybe you would do a better job of juggling crumbling walls, woodworm-munched beams, missing roof tiles, and raging squirrels. Miss Bunsen is a hero," Halinka said, looking at Pearl for backup.

Pearl stepped in between her two quarreling friends.

"Listen, we are in this situation now, and it doesn't matter how we got here. The important thing is that we need to get out, and we need to get back to school and find out who has the Tome and get it back!"

Millie slumped down against the wall and sat on the floor, pulling a copy of *Mechanical*

Matrix Monthly out of her bag.

"Millie," Pearl said. "What are you doing? Aren't we going to put our heads together and get out of here, like we always do? Come on, we're Bunseners, right?"

Millie looked up from her magazine, glared at Halinka, then looked back down at the pages.

Pearl rolled her eyes. "Come on, you two! There must be a vent or an opening in this room somewhere. The candles are lit, so there's an oxygen source somewhere."

Neither of her friends said anything. Pearl looked at them despairingly. This had never happened before—not in such a serious way.

"Halinka?" Pearl said hopefully. "Do you want to help here?"

"Not really," Halinka said in a put-on haughty voice as she stared at Millie. "If Millie thinks she's so much better than everyone else, she can figure out how to get us out of here without my help."

"I do not think I'm better than everyone else!" Millie interrupted, jumping to her feet.

"I'm off," Halinka snorted, turning on her heel and stomping to the other end of the room.

"STOP RIGHT THERE!" Millie shouted, causing the entire school, including Miss Bunsen, to turn and look.

Halinka stopped in her tracks, completely taken aback by her usually quiet friend's second outburst of the day.

"Millie, it's okay. We'll fix this. It's okay," Pearl said desperately, rushing toward her friend before Millie could do anything too rash. Pearl had never seen Millie's face so flushed.

"No," Millie said, and a huge smile spread across her face. "I meant, stop actually *right there.*"

"I'm stopped—now explain!" Halinka said. She was ready to keep storming off at any moment.

"Now step back three steps, stomping like you were," Millie ordered.

Halinka stomped back three paces.

"Now stomp back another three."

Halinka's eyes narrowed suspiciously, but she did as Millie said.

"Did you hear that?"

"Hear what?" Pearl whispered, worried her friend was going slightly mad.

"The difference in sound!" Halinka shouted, dropping to the floor and patting it.

Millie ran over with her flashlight and shone it where Halinka was kneeling.

"There—look! A latch!" she said excitedly.

"Come on, Pearl, help us open it!"

The whole school crowded around to watch as Halinka heaved open a trapdoor, revealing a narrow flight of stairs leading into darkness.

Pearl, Halinka, and Millie directed each Bunsener to grab a candle and start climbing down the stairs. After everyone else had gone, Pearl shimmied through the hatch, followed by Halinka, while Millie held the trapdoor open. But Miss Bunsen was still standing in the corner, having made no move to try to escape.

"Miss Bunsen, come on! Before the creepy voice comes back and catches us escaping!" Millie called out to her teacher. Miss Bunsen seemed to shake herself out of her trance and slowly moved toward the hatch.

Millie held out her hand and helped Miss Bunsen down the steps before shutting the trapdoor tight above their heads.

Chapter 8

"There better not be any squirrels down here!" Halinka said. She jerkily moved her candle from left to right, lighting up the tunnel walls.

"I can see light up ahead," Pearl said over her shoulder.

"Thank grommets for that," Millie said, holding her nose. "I think Brains has let off a real stinker."

It wasn't long before the students reached the end of the tunnel. Miss Bunsen was the last to climb up into the daylight. She straightened her glasses and cleared her throat.

"Girls, I have let you down immeasurably."

A symphony of "nos" and "of course you haven'ts" came from the schoolgirls, and before she could even finish her sentence, she was surrounded by her beloved Bunseners.

"You could never let us down, Miss Bunsen," said Pearl. The rest of the students nodded vigorously in agreement.

"Well, nod then!" Halinka said, nudging Millie. But Millie was still stone-faced.

Miss Bunsen dabbed her eyes with her handkerchief before raising her head high. "Miss Bunsen's School for Brilliant Girls will *not* be bulldozed!" she shouted. "The Tome of Thought, which has been resident at the school since its birth, will be *retrieved!*"

The whole school clapped and cheered wildly as Miss Bunsen marched off toward the school bus, motioning for her girls to follow.

"All aboard?" Miss Bunsen shouted.

"Yes, miss!" came the reply in unison.

"Then let this battle begin!" Miss Bunsen said. She turned the key in the ignition, only to hear a faint whirring sound.

"Let this battle begin!" she said again, enthusiastically trying the ignition for a second time. This time, there was no sound at all.

"Oh dear," she said to Brains, who was sitting next to her on the front seat.

"What's the matter?" Pearl asked from right behind them. She, Millie, and Halinka had traded their cool back-row seats for the front row to be closer to Miss Bunsen.

"I fear I may have forgotten to fill the old girl up," Miss Bunsen said cheerfully.

Pearl wasn't sure how Miss Bunsen could remain cheerful. They had to get back to the school to save it! She looked at Millie and Halinka, who seemed equally confused.

"Well," Miss Bunsen said as she flipped various levers and switches on the bus's dashboard, "there's only one thing for it!"

"A walk to the gas station?" Halinka suggested.

"No, my dear." Miss Bunsen chuckled. "We must hoist the mast! I told you we Bunseners do things our own way. Follow me."

Pearl, Halinka, and Millie followed her up

the spiral staircase to the upper deck of the bus. They watched as their ingenious head-mistress moved schoolgirls out of the way and folded their seats toward the bus's walls.

"Why are you three just standing there? Come on, help!"

When most of the seats on the top deck were folded to the side, a hatch the length of the bus became visible in the floor.

"All together, now. Let's pull this open!"

Pearl, Halinka, Millie, and some of the other Bunseners heaved open the trapdoor to reveal a shiny wooden mast, complete with beautiful red sails.

"Here," Miss Bunsen said, tossing ropes to Pearl, Halinka, and Millie. "Go and tie these jiggers to the stern. Then pull the jib over to the bow and secure it to the bowsprit."

The girls ran to the back and

then to the front of the bus and pulled on the ropes. They watched in awe as the mast began to rise up above the bus.

"Pull harder on the jib!" Miss Bunsen shouted as the wind began to pick up again. She threw another rope to two Bunseners at the bow of the bus. "Now, heave!"

The bus began to slowly judder as the bright-red sails started to flap in the stormy sky.

"Right! Someone needs to steer this old girl, so I'll leave you lot to it!"

"Wait!" Pearl called out. "We don't know how to sail!"

"You will by the time we get back to school!" Miss Bunsen hollered up the stairs. "All part of the curriculum, my dear!"

Pearl, Halinka, and Millie took control of the ropes and maneuvered the sails so that they caught the wind.

"This is by far the best lesson we've ever had!" Halinka said, tugging on the rope, imagining she was a pirate on the high seas.

"And the most dangerous!" Millie shrieked as she tried to keep her feet on the deck so as not to be blown away.

"At least it's not raining anymore!" Pearl said. She ducked her head as the boom swung starboard.

"Hang on, why aren't we moving?" Halinka asked, licking her finger and holding it up to the wind. "Aye, it be blowy enough."

Pearl laughed. "You're right, matey!"

"I think I know what the problem might be," Millie said, rolling her eyes. Pearl and Halinka caught on quickly.

"Take your foot off the brake!" the three shouted together.

"Sorry!" came Miss Bunsen's voice from belowdecks.

The bus suddenly jumped into motion. It moved forward, then lurched over to one side.

Everyone on the bus screamed. It seemed their voyage was over before it had even begun.

"Whoops! Nearly forgot the stabilizers!"

Miss Bunsen flicked a switch above her head and waited as the back wheels of the bus extended out on their axles to stop it from tipping over.

They set off again, sailing slowly at first but gathering speed quickly. Soon they were gliding along the country roads back to school.

"I hope Miss Bunsen has chosen the route avoiding the low bridge," Millie said.

"Perhaps you should give Miss Bunsen a little more credit, Millie," Halinka said, pulling on the sail ropes.

"I didn't mean anything bad," said Millie with a shrug, pulling equally hard on her side of the sail. "I was just saying I hope she remembered."

"You're pulling too hard," Halinka snapped.

"I think you'll find you are the one pulling too hard the *wrong way*. In case you neglected to notice, the breeze is blowing in an easterly direction. I should be pulling my way."

Pearl watched her two best friends pull and tug at the ropes. The bus flailed from one side of the road to the other.

"Do you think we need to talk about this?" Pearl finally cried, grabbing both sets of ropes to steady the bus.

"Talk about what?" Halinka huffed.

Millie tutted and looked out at the passing scenery.

"About you two. You've been bickering this whole trip."

"Well, it's not my fault Little Miss Logical has to be a complete know-it-all." Halinka said, tilting her head and pursing her lips.

"I am not a know-it-all," Millie protested. "I just like things done the right way."

"Who's to say what the right way is, and what it isn't?" replied Halinka.

"Why are you even bothered?" Millie asked, genuinely confused. "I haven't said anything about you or the way you do things. I've only been talking about Miss Bunsen."

"Okay, listen!" Pearl suddenly chirped. "You are both so caught up in this that you can't see each other's point of view."

Halinka and Millie looked at their friend, still hanging on tightly to their ropes.

"Millie," Pearl said, looking at her friend with compassion, "sometimes when you say something about a person, it can upset other people too."

"How so? That's ridiculous."

"For example, when you said that you felt

Miss Bunsen was wrong to let her emotions override her logic, that upset Halinka and hurt her feelings."

"It did?" Millie said, looking worried. "But how? I didn't mean to hurt your feelings, Halinka. Is that why you've been so angry with me?"

"Because," Pearl continued, "Halinka is passionate, feisty, and a ball of emotional energy. She, too, puts her feelings in front of logic sometimes, and sometimes that is the right thing to do."

Millie thought for a moment. "Like when she realized we had to spell the symbol for neon backward because of the neon sign. She didn't use logic. She went beyond logic."

"Exactly! And you worked together using logic and emotion to solve the task."

"And when we were trapped," Halinka said, "and I got all emotional and stomped off, your logic helped us find the hidden trapdoor."

"But we wouldn't have necessarily found it without your emotional outburst," Millie mused.

The three friends all looked at one another and smiled.

"Bridge!" came a scream from the bow of the bus.

"Quick, pull down the sail!" Pearl shouted as the Bunseners all frantically hoisted the ropes and pulled the mast down, just in time for the bus to whoosh underneath the arched railway bridge and make its way through the last village before reaching Miss Bunsen's School.

"I wonder what will be left of the school when we arrive," Millie said as she helped Halinka hoist the mast and sails back up.

"I don't know," Halinka said in a serious tone. "But we are Bunseners. Even if everything is gone, we'll find a way to rebuild."

"And wherever the Tome of Thought has gone," said Pearl, "we'll find it. I mean, we have an army of squirrels, right? Those fluffy detectives can find anything!"

Chapter 9

"School ahoy!" Miss Bunsen trilled. "Get ready to disembark!"

The bus glided slowly down the hill toward the school and then suddenly jerked to a stop.

Pearl, Halinka, and Millie clattered down the stairs to find Miss Bunsen peering through a telescope at the school, which had just come into view.

"What is it, Miss Bunsen?" Millie asked. "Why have we stopped?"

"I've decided to be a bit more cautious about

things. Maybe I shouldn't just rush into situations without checking them out a little first," she said, smiling at the girls.

She handed the telescope to Halinka. "What can you see?"

"There are no bulldozers or excavators," Halinka reported as she peered through the lens.

"And the school is still completely intact?" Millie asked. The entire bus listened intently.

"Yes, it's all still in one piece."

"I guess the creepy voice kept its word," Pearl said.

"No, it's not good. Something isn't right, but I can't quite put my finger on it," Halinka said as she peered out the windshield of the bus.

Miss Bunsen stood up from the driver's seat

and grabbed Brains.

"Girls, you must all wait here and stay safe  while I go and investigate the situation."

"We'll come with you, Miss Bunsen," Millie said, taking her teacher by the hand. "And I just wanted to say thank you for being so wonderful."

"Not now, Millie dear! This is no time to be getting all emotional!" Miss Bunsen said, pulling her black cape up over her shoulders.

Millie looked at Halinka and Pearl and shrugged.

"Come on, then," Miss Bunsen said. "I need you three. Pearl, Halinka, and Millie."

The remaining Bunseners all piled to one

side of the bus as they watched Miss Bunsen and the girls sneakily walk up the hill, then hide behind the gatehouse.

"Look," Millie said, pointing up to the roof of the school. "It looks like someone has fixed the loose slates."

"And repointed the chimney!" said Pearl.

"And check out the assembly hall!" Halinka said. "All the broken glass has been replaced in the windows."

"This is very weird," said Pearl, pulling her goggles down to have a better look. "I thought the school was going to be destroyed, not renovated!"

"What can you see, Pearl?" Miss Bunsen asked nervously.

"I'm just fixing my heat-sensing lens. It will work in a sec, hang on."

There was silence as Pearl twiddled buttons and focused her lens on her goggles.

"There!" she suddenly said. "There are three figures in your office, Miss Bunsen."

"Can you see who they are?" Miss Bunsen said, fiddling with her pearls.

"No, all I can see are white figures."

"Human figures?" Millie asked.

"Well, they're too big to be squirrels!" Pearl said.

"Apart from those three,

are there any other sources of heat in the school?" Miss Bunsen asked.

"No, it's all clear."

Miss Bunsen and the girls crept through the schoolyard and in through the front doors, which were freshly painted with bright-white paint.

They edged their way along the walls, creeping along the corridors, which all looked like they had been recently mopped.

"This is so weird," Millie said.

"I know. The vending machine used to be right here, and now it's not!" Halinka replied.

"I think Millie is suggesting that the whole situation is a bit weird," Pearl said helpfully.

Just as Halinka pulled a half-eaten and slightly moldy granola bar out of her pocket, her tummy let out a loud grumble.

"Halinka! Stop your tummy from making all that noise!" Millie squeaked. "And put that back in your pocket. Now is no time to be eating!"

The group quietly crept along the wet floor until they were at the bottom of the stairs to Miss Bunsen's attic office.

They creaked their way up the crooked steps.

"Okay, girls, this is it!" Miss Bunsen whispered before kung-fu kicking open her office door.

Miss Bunsen, Pearl, Halinka, and Millie couldn't believe their eyes at who was sitting behind Miss Bunsen's desk.

"Darlings! How nice of you to drop in. I wondered how long it would be before we had a visit."

Miss Bunsen and her girls watched as Miss Acid, her high-heeled feet slung up on the desk, leafed lazily through the Tome of Thought

with her overly manicured hands. Megan and Heather, Atom Academy's top troublemakers, were behind her, looking through interior design magazines.

"I knew it!" Millie seethed. "Atom Academy girls are never far away when there is trouble."

"What are you doing here in my school?" Miss Bunsen said, puffing out her chest and putting her hands on her hips.

Miss Acid let out a slow trickle of a laugh that sounded like nails being dragged down a chalkboard. "You poor, pathetic creature. Your school? How sweet. This is my school now."

Pearl, Halinka, and Millie all huddled in close to Miss Bunsen, who put her arms around them.

"You see, ladies, this school has something." Miss Acid stood up and walked toward them with the Tome in her hands, her perfectly tailored dress shimmering in the low evening light. "I don't know what it is that makes this school special—maybe it's this funny little book—but I know it's not you."

Miss Acid popped her finger on Miss Bunsen's nose. "So you must be gone, along with all your scruffy little Bunseners. Whatever energy this school has, whatever power enables it to win every single competition with virtually no equipment—well, I want that power."

"You can't have it!" Halinka shouted, lurching forward toward Miss Acid.

"Careful, my little feisty one. You wouldn't want to get grubby hand marks all over my nice dress, would you?"

Megan and Heather laughed and snorted.

"Ugh, I'm bored with this now," Miss Acid suddenly said before clapping her hands three times. Five Grrl Bots flew into the room.

"Oh, not the Grrl Bots!" Pearl grimaced as the tiny flying robots that had been programmed to be mean buzzed around their heads.

"I'm guessing they're responsible for cleaning up our school," Halinka said.

"They might be mean, but they sure know how to fix stuff up! And their outfits are pretty

cute too." Millie admired their metallic white dresses and pretty wings.

"Tie them up, Grrls," Miss Acid snarled, "while I figure out what to do with them. Oh, and send a crew of Bots to find the bus. It must be hiding around here somewhere with all the other bedraggled wretches on board."

The Grrl Bots flew into action and tied Miss Bunsen, Pearl, Halinka, Millie, and Brains up with the fronds of the giant pumpkin plants that lined the office.

"Come on, Megan and Heather. We need to go and decide where we're going to install the Jacuzzi."

Megan and Heather jumped to it and began clip-clopping their fancy boots across the attic floor, following Miss Acid out the attic door.

"One more thing," Miss Bunsen called out. "I have a question for you."

"Oh, hurry up then, what is it?" Miss Acid sighed.

"Why such an elaborate trick? Why the maze, the warehouse, all that effort?"

Miss Acid turned to face Miss Bunsen.

"I knew you would do anything for money to mend your tatty old school. I also knew that I had to get you all out of here to empty the place. You might be naive, Miss Bunsen, but your girls are not, so whatever trick I used had to be believable enough to give me time to install my Grrl Bots. I had to keep you all there without anyone smelling a rat. To be honest, I didn't expect you to escape so quickly."

Miss Acid spun back around and walked out of the room, leaving Miss Bunsen and her girls tied up alone in the attic.

Chapter 10

"Now what?" Halinka asked, wriggling about. "Can we get out from these pumpkin fronds?"

"No, dear, not a chance," Miss Bunsen said woefully. "I've been feeding them squirrel poo all summer long. They will be extra strong."

"We need to do something, and quickly," Millie said. "The rest of the students are still on the bus, and it's only a matter of time before the Grrl Bots find them."

"You're right," Miss Bunsen replied. "Anyone got any good ideas?"

"I have." Pearl smiled. "I've learned a lot from watching Millie and Halinka and their ingenious invention of the Rube Goldberg machine. I think we can use what we've learned."

"But how? We're in a bit of a pumpkin bind here!" Millie squeaked.

"Allow me!" Halinka said as she wriggled her hand down into her pocket and pulled out the remnants of her moldy granola bar.

"Heeeeere, squirrels, come to Linky."

Millie's eyes widened as at least two dozen fluffy fiends surrounded the trapped group.

"Now nibble Linky and her friends free, and you can have Linky's 'nola bar."

Pearl and Millie looked at Halinka. "You can talk to squirrels?" Millie said in shock.

"I thought you hated squirrels!" Pearl added.

"Sssshhhh!" Halinka hissed. "Do you want to get out of here or not?"

The squirrels gnawed through the pumpkin vines and set the girls and Miss Bunsen free,

then held out their paws. Halinka gave each squirrel a piece of granola bar and some money for the vending machine.

The girls hugged, glad to be free.

"Your squirrel-whispering skills certainly came in handy, Halinka," Millie said.

"And now we need to fall upon your skills," Halinka replied.

"I just love it when my Bunseners put their creative minds together! My dears, what is your plan?" asked Miss Bunsen.

Pearl smiled knowingly. "Oh, I think you'll get the gist pretty quickly."

She began to gather all manner of bits and bobs from around Miss Bunsen's office. Dominoes, teacups, marbles, old seed packets, watering cans, paper clips, and anything else she could find.

Millie drew out a diagram on the back of one of Miss Bunsen's many overdue bills, while Halinka and Pearl arranged all the pieces of the trap as she had designed it.

Halinka pulled out her gum and fixed the last component into place. It was a stapler, fully loaded and ready to fire its pointy artillery.

Miss Bunsen, Pearl, Halinka, Millie, and Brains all ducked down and hid behind a giant pumpkin in the corner.

"Now all we have to do is wait." Pearl smiled.

It wasn't long before the sound of Miss Acid's high heels, followed by Megan and Heather's tottering footsteps, sounded up the attic stairs.

The attic door opened, and the three Atom Academy trespassers walked in. They tripped over a wire that triggered the first domino to fall over, setting off the trap's sequence of events.

"What is going on? Where are those Bunseners?" screamed Miss Acid as the line of dominoes collapsed one on top of another, leading to an orange that rolled down some guttering, landing on the stapler, which then shot off a spray of staples.

There was a loud squeak, followed by a thundering of tiny, squirrelly paws.

"Yes!" Pearl quietly punched the air. "It worked!"

"Right in the bottom!" Halinka laughed as the angry squirrel pulled a staple out of its backside.

The irate squirrel mob descended upon Miss Acid, Heather, and Megan, causing them to flail about helplessly in an attempt to swat the fluffy assassins off.

The trap's sequence continued.

Megan stumbled backward and knocked over a bucket of tea, causing a hollowed-out pumpkin to fall from above and cover her head.

Heather staggered about, her face covered in squirrels, only to step on a book that was attached to a spring that was attached to a brush that was hovering above Miss Bunsen's best laying chicken, Miss Isle.

"Why is your chicken called Miss Isle?" Millie asked Miss Bunsen as they watched the chaos from behind their pumpkin hideout.

Miss Bunsen chuckled. "Because when you brush her back, she lays eggs, and they shoot out like missiles."

The brush slowly lowered and began to brush the hen's back, and Miss Isle let out a happy little clucking sound. Realizing what was about to happen, the squirrels on Heather's head scattered as egg after egg shot out of Miss Isle and splattered all

over Heather.

Finally, Miss Acid, having flung the last squirrel away, ran for the door.

"Not so fast." Millie smirked as she punched a code into the keyboard linked to Miss Bunsen's computer.

The great window of Miss Bunsen's office smashed into a thousand pieces as hundreds of Grrl Bots, all re-programmed to capture

the Atomers, flew in and grabbed Miss Acid by her lapels. Other bots grabbed Heather and Megan and swooped them all out the door, back off to Atom Academy.

The dust settled, and the Bunseners emerged from their hiding place. They crunched over the broken glass that was all over the floor.

"The Tome of Thought!" Miss Bunsen suddenly said, turning around frantically to look for the precious book.

"Um," Halinka said, "I think I've found it...or rather, Brains did." She held up the Tome with two fingers, holding her nose.

"Oh dear," Miss Bunsen said with a laugh. "I'm sure it will dry out!"

Chapter 11

By the next morning, the rain clouds had blown away, and Pearl, Halinka, and Millie were in the school cafeteria having an early breakfast of eggs and toast.

"Well, thank you very much, Miss Isle," Pearl said, stroking the chicken that was snuggled up on her knee. "That egg was delicious!"

Miss Isle let out a happy cluck.

"It feels so good to be sitting here having breakfast and not look up to see the sky through the roof!" Millie said, gazing at the mended tiles that had been perfectly patched into place.

"I don't know," Halinka mused. "I kind of miss the old school. It had character."

"Well, I'd trade character for a dry head anytime," Millie replied.

"I guess you two have opposite opinions about pretty much everything!" Pearl laughed.

"I feel like I've learned a lot over this last adventure, though," Millie said, looking up shyly.

"I think I know what you mean," Halinka replied. She reached over and topped off her friend's teacup with more tea.

"Care to elaborate?" Pearl asked, sitting back in her chair and waiting to see who would be the first to speak. Her friends both opened their mouths at the same time, then laughed.

"I guess sometimes I can be a little square and a bit close-minded," Millie said, taking a sip of her tea. "A bit, well, too buttoned up and always going by the book." She looked at Halinka. "I get how that must be a little frustrating sometimes, especially when we're on one of our adventures and we never know what's going to happen next."

"And I've realized that I can be a little, well, crazy sometimes," Halinka said, plopping six sugar cubes into her tea. "I like to figure stuff out my own way and don't always want to abide by what it says I have to do in some textbook somewhere. And I know sometimes that can get me into trouble—but sometimes it gets me, and us, out of trouble too."

Pearl leaned forward, placing her hands upon her friends' hands.

"And do you know what? That's how you guys work so well together. Like anything in this universe with two opposite ends—"

"Like the North Pole and the South Pole!" Halinka said.

"And positive and negative energy!" Millie clapped her hands.

"—opposites attract!" Pearl said, moving the sugar bowl away from Halinka.

"I spent all night cleaning the Tome," Millie said. She pulled the crinkly-paged book out of her bag. "It still smells of wee a little, but I sprayed some perfume on each page, and that's masking it just about enough!"

The girls laughed.

"Anyway, I found this passage and wanted to read it to you guys." Millie opened the Tome to where she had marked it with a ribbon.

In our world, differences are the key to

life as we know it.

Our universe is a mass of opposite energies,

Without which our solar system would

stop turning.

Millie closed the Tome and smiled.

"I love our little universe here at Miss Bunsen's."

"Me too." Halinka said.

"And me," Pearl added. "But wait—look at the squirrels!"

Halinka and Millie looked up at their fluffy audience, who were dabbing their eyes with napkins on the rafters high above the cafeteria.

"Talk about being over-emotional!" Millie said with a wink before slinging her bag over her shoulder and jumping up out of her seat.

"Come on, we're all going to be late for our first class."

The three friends gathered their things and skipped off to their first lesson, excited for what the day ahead would bring.

Don't miss Pearl, Millie, and Halinka's first adventures!

Can a great idea put
Miss Bunsen's school a
head above the rest?

Pearl, Millie,
and Halinka shoot
for the stars!

978-0-8075-5157-8 HC
978-0-8075-5154-7 PB
978-0-8075-5156-1 eBook

978-0-8075-5158-5 HC
978-0-8075-5153-0 PB
978-0-8075-5155-4 eBook